Hello, Family Members,

Learning to read is one of the most important accomplishments of early childhood. **Hello Reader!** books are designed to help children become skilled readers who like to read. Beginning readers learn to read by remembering frequently used words like "the," "is," and "and"; by using phonics skills to decode new words; and by interpreting picture and text clues. These books provide both the stories children enjoy and the structure they need to read fluently and independently. Here are suggestions for helping your child *before*, *during*, and *after* reading:

Before

- Look at the cover and pictures and have your child predict what the story is about.
- Read the story to your child.
- Encourage your child to chime in with familiar words and phrases.
- Echo read with your child by reading a line first and having your child read it after you do.

During

- Have your child think about a word he or she does not recognize right away. Provide hints such as "Let's see if we know the sounds" and "Have we read other words like this one?"
- Encourage your child to use phonics skills to sound out new words.
- Provide the word for your child when more assistance is needed so that he or she does not struggle and the experience of reading with you is a positive one.
- Encourage your child to have fun by reading with a lot of expression . . . like an actor!

After

- Have your child keep lists of interesting and favorite words.
- Encourage your child to read the books over and over again. Have him or her read to brothers, sisters, grandparents, and even teddy bears. Repeated readings develop confidence in young readers.
- Talk about the stories. Ask and answer questions. Share ideas about the funniest and most interesting characters and events in the stories.

I do hope that you and your child enjoy this book.

—Francie Alexander
Reading Specialist,
Scholastic's Learning Ventures

W9-AXR-455

For Kim and Robert

Copyright © 1968 by Norman Bridwell; copyright © renewed 1996 Norman Bridwell. All rights reserved. Published by Scholastic Inc. SCHOLASTIC, HELLO READER! and CARTWHEEL BOOKS and associated logos are trademarks and/or registered trademarks of Scholastic Inc.

Library of Congress Cataloging-in-Publication Data

Bridwell, Norman.
     A tiny family / by Norman Bridwell.
       p.   cm.— (Hello reader! Level 1)
     "Cartwheel Books."
     Summary: A tiny girl and her tiny brother embark on a perilous journey into the house of a giant to retrieve their grandfather's umbrella.
     ISBN 0-439-04019-1
     [1. Fairies—Fiction. 2. Brothers and sisters—Fiction.]
I. Title. II. Series.
PZ7.B7633Ti   1999
[E]—dc21
                           98-8689
                           CIP
                           AC

10 9   0/0 01 02 03 04

Printed in the U.S.A.   **14**
First printing, March 1999

NORMAN BRIDWELL

A Tiny Family

Hello Reader! — Level 1

SCHOLASTIC INC.

Cartwheel BOOKS®

New York Toronto London Auckland Sydney

Hello. I'm a tiny girl.
I live with my tiny family in a garden.
Our home is under the flowers.

Every morning we have breakfast —
corn flakes and a strawberry.

Then my brother and I wash
the clothes.

We help Grandpa gather
the vegetables.

Then we all do the cooking.

After the work is done,
I like to play leapfrog.

My brother likes to slide.

We both like to climb.
One day we climbed
to the top of the tallest
flower in the garden.

I looked all around.
I saw something scary!

A giant girl was sitting near our garden.
She was talking to a giant dog.
There was something stuck in his paw.

It was Grandpa's umbrella!
The dog must have stepped on it.

"What a pretty little umbrella!"
said the girl.
And she ran to her house with it.

We had to get Grandpa's
umbrella back.
So that night, when Grandpa was
sleeping, my brother and I got up.

We left the garden and went
up the hill to the house
where the giant girl lived.

We didn't go in the front door.

But we found an open window
Up we climbed.

The girl was fast asleep.
Grandpa's umbrella was
on the table.

I thought I could swing
over to the table.

But I was wrong.

My brother slid down the curtain
and helped me out.
How could we get up on that table?
I had an idea.

We could build steps up
to the top of the table.

We used all the blocks.

Oops!

My brother brought me
a giant whistle.

We climbed up the whistle
and I grabbed the umbrella.

Just then —

— the giant girl picked me up.
Oh, I was scared!

She opened her mouth.
"Who are you?" she asked.

I told her about us.
I told her that we had come
to get Grandpa's umbrella.

She was very kind.
She gave us the umbrella
and said she would take us
back to our garden.

And she did.

Then we went to sleep and dreamed about giant people.